GRUNT

For Huw and William

A RED FOX BOOK: 0 09 943407 5

Published in Great Britain by Red Fox,
An imprint of Random House Children's Books

PRINTING HISTORY
This edition published 2002

1 3 5 7 9 10 8 6 4 2

Text © John Richardson 2002

The right of John Richardson
to be identified as the author and illustrator of this work
has been asserted in accordance with the
Copyright, Designs and Patents Act 1988

RANDOM HOUSE CHILDREN'S BOOKS
61–63 Uxbridge Rd, London W5 5SA
A division of The Random House Group Ltd

RANDOM HOUSE AUSTRALIA (PTY) LTD
20 Alfred Street, Milsons Point, Sydney,
New South Wales 2061, Australia

RANDOM HOUSE NEW ZEALAND LTD
18 Poland Road, Glenfield, Auckland 10, New Zealand

RANDOM HOUSE (PTY) LTD
Endulini, 5A Jubilee Road, Parktown 2193, South Africa

THE RANDOM HOUSE GROUP Limited Reg. No. 954009
www.randomhouse.co.uk

A CIP catalogue record for this book is available from the British Library.

Printed and bound in Singapore by Tien Wah Press

GRUNT

JOHN RICHARDSON

RED FOX

A whiskery pig and his fine fat wife had six piglets.
The last and the least they called Wee-skin-and-bones.

This little piggy had crinkly-crumply ears, a tiddly-widdly button of a snout and absolutely no tail at all. And when he tried to squeal, all that came out was a teeny-tiny grunt.

His brothers and sisters, however, were big, beautiful, plump piggies with flippy-flappy ears, big snuffly-snorty snouts and curly-whirly tails. But they were unkind to their tiny brother.

'He's not playing with us!' they squealed.

'He's got no tail to wiggle and squiggle.'

'His snout is too small to snuffle and truffle.'

'His ears don't go flippety-flappety.'

'He's just a Wee-skin-and-bones.'

The whiskery papa pig didn't seem to notice him at all.
But what made Wee-skin and-bones especially sad was
that his brothers and sisters made so much noise his
mama couldn't hear his tiny grunts.

'Nobody loves me,' sobbed Wee-skin-and-bones.

'Cock-a-doodle-do! What'll little piggy do?' crowed the rooster.

'Me-oh-my! He can't stay in the sty,' bleated the sheep.

'Neigh-neigh-neigh! You must go away!' cried the horse.

'Off you go then,' said the fat speckled hen.

So Wee-skin-and-bones ran wee-wee-wee all the way from home until he reached the middle of a great dark forest.

High above him, the cold moon shone in the black night sky.

He thought about his warm bed of straw. He thought about his brothers and sisters. He thought about his mama and papa.

And he cried a whole puddle of tears.

An owl hooted. Leaves rustled.
Wee-skin-and-bones rubbed his
eyes and looked hard into the shadows.
Two beady eyes looked back at him.
'What's the matter, little piggy?' asked a
wonderfully kind voice.
'I'm Wee-skin-and-bones and I'm all alone in the
big wide world.'
'Then it's good that I'm here,' said the voice. 'My name
is Old-scratch-and-scruff. I'm a bristly old scruff on the outside,
but inside… Oooo… I'm a BEAUTY! Will you be my friend?'

'Me! How can I be your friend?' sighed Wee-skin-and-bones, 'when I have no tail to wiggle and squiggle?'

'Tails?' said Old-scratch-and-scruff. 'I can take 'em or leave 'em.'

'But my ears are all crinkly and crumply, I've got a tiddly-widdly snout and no one can hear my teeny-tiny grunt.'

'Crinkly! Crumply! Tiddly! Widdly!' cried Old-scratch-and-scruff. 'Wonderful, couldn't be better. And I can hear you just fine.'

Old-scratch-and-scruff led the little piggy to the warmth and safety of his den. He gave him supper and then tucked him up in a bed of moss and leaves.

'Good night, Wee-skin-and-bones,' whispered the scruffy boar.

In the morning, Old-scratch-and-scruff took
Wee-skin-and-bones for a romp through
the forest. They jumped in puddles. They
chased the leaves on the breeze.

They snuffled for truffles.

They pulled
plums off the trees.

Suddenly, Wee-skin-and-bones let out such a big grunt that he startled Old-scratch and scruff. 'What's this feeling I've got?' he gasped. 'Like…'

'Like you've a tail that's curly and whirly?' said
Old-scratch-and-scruff.

'And, like my ears are flippy-flappy. And my snout is
all snuffly and snorty,' finished Wee-skin-and-bones.

'That's happy!' cried Old-scratch-and-scruff. 'Happy inside out!'

'But…' said the little piggy.

'There's something missing…?' finished the boar.

'Yes,' said Wee-skin-and-bones.

All of a sudden, there was a great snorting and snuffling and squeaking and squealing. Wee-skin-and-bones' mama came trundling up the hill, with her babies following close behind.

She took one look at Wee-skin-and-bones and burst into a
whole torrent of tears.

'There you are!' she cried. 'I've been searching
everywhere for you.'

'Oh,' said Wee-skin-and-bones, 'you don't mind
that I'm all tiddly-widdly and crinkly-crumply?'

'Crinkly-crumply, tiddly-widdly… is even more precious,' said the fine mama pig, smothering her baby in a whole shower of kisses.

'GRUNT!' cried Wee-skin-and-bones very loudly and happily.

'My thoughts exactly!' cried Old-scratch-and-scruff,
as he quietly slipped back into the forest.